D1096101

in the
news™

HURRICANES

Paul Kupperberg

ROSEN
PUBLISHING®

New York

Published in 2007 by The Rosen Publishing Group, Inc.
29 East 21st Street, New York, NY 10010

Copyright © 2007 by The Rosen Publishing Group, Inc.

First Edition

Library of Congress Cataloging-in-Publication Data

Kupperberg, Paul.
Hurricanes / Paul Kupperberg.—1st ed.
    p. cm.—(In the news)
Includes bibliographical references and index.
ISBN-13: 978-1-4042-0974-9 (lib. bdg.)
ISBN-10: 1-4042-0974-3 (lib. bdg.)
1. Hurricanes. 2. Typhoons. I. Title.
QC944.K87 2007
363.34'922—dc22
2006024495

Manufactured in the United States of America

On the cover: Top, left: A man is rescued from his home in New Orleans, Louisiana, in the aftermath of Hurricane Katrina in 2005; Top, right: Sun streams in through the torn roof of the New Orleans Superdome, which served as an emergency shelter for thousands of city residents following the massive flooding caused by Hurricane Katrina; Bottom, left: Hurricane Frances blasts against palm trees and seawall in Lantana Beach, Florida, in 2004; Bottom, right: An aerial view taken from a Coast Guard helicopter of the flooded streets of New Orleans in the wake of Hurricane Katrina.

contents

The Science of Hurricanes

Imagine a force of nature so powerful that it can peel back the roof of a building as easily as you tear open a box of cereal. A force so great that everything it cannot sweep from its path, it simply smashes through or flattens. A force that generates a wind so powerful, it has been known to drive a piece of plywood straight through a tree trunk.

All this destructive force is contained in a massive, swirling, erratically moving system of clouds, moisture, and static electricity that can pick up as much as two billion tons of water a day through evaporation and sea spray as it travels across the ocean. This weather system can be from 200 to 500 miles (322 to 805 kilometers) wide and bring with it torrential rains and killer winds in excess of 140 mph (225 km/h). The entire system moves over ocean and land at speeds averaging 12 mph (19 km/h) or more. If all its power could be harnessed, it would release enough energy to supply the United States with electricity for almost a year, or the equivalent explosive energy of about 400 twenty-megaton hydrogen bombs (a megaton is equal to the force of one million tons of conventional explosives).

A satellite captured 1985's Hurricane Elena as it gathered strength in the Gulf of Mexico.

To the people living along the Indian Ocean and near Australia, this force is called a cyclone, while in Indonesia it is called a baguio. It is known as a typhoon in the western Pacific. In the rest of the Pacific Ocean, the Atlantic Ocean, and the Caribbean, this force of nature is called a hurricane. Meteorologists call it a tropical cyclone. Unlike other natural disasters, the relatively slow-moving development of hurricanes gives ample warning of their approach.

A hurricane specialist tracks the first named storm of 2006—Tropical Storm Alberto—as it heads toward Florida.

But unlike the sudden onslaught of earthquakes, floods, and landslides, they can move slowly, giving their high winds and lashing rains lots of time to destroy everything they encounter.

During the last decade, according to the National Hurricane Center, hurricane season along the eastern seaboard of the United States, which runs from June 1 to November 30, has averaged fifteen named tropical storms, eight named hurricanes, and four major hurricanes a year (a tropical storm is given a name such as

"Alberto" or "Bertha" once it reaches a certain strength). The 2005 season was the most destructive in recorded history (reliable weather records date back to 1851), with twenty-eight named storms, fifteen hurricanes, and seven intense hurricanes.

The cause for the increase in hurricane activity is a subject of sharp debate. Some attribute the upswing in the number, intensity, and destructiveness of storms to such factors as global warming, erosion to coastal areas due to development, and diverse meteorological reasons, including high-altitude wind currents. Others believe that the current severe weather is just part of a natural twenty-year cycle.

Whatever the cause, the federal and state governments are taking the threat of increased storm activity very seriously. Efforts to increase the reliability of hurricane forecasting and tracking technology are underway. Plans are also being put in place to improve the reaction time and procedures of various emergency responders and relief agencies that will be called upon in the next emergency that is sure to strike the Atlantic or Gulf Coasts of the United States.

The islands of the Caribbean and the entire eastern seaboard and Gulf Coast of the United States sit in the path of these monster storms. For all who live there, the question is not if they will ever again be caught in a hurricane's monstrous fury, but when.

It Starts as a Tropical Wave

The word "hurricane" is derived from the Spanish word *huracan*, which means "great wind." But before the great wind can ever gather its destructive might, a hurricane begins as nothing more than sunshine that evaporates large amounts of seawater after warming the surface of the tropical oceans along the earth's equator to temperatures above 80 degrees Fahrenheit (27 degrees Celsius). The equator is the latitude line (running east to west) around the middle of the planet and at which the earth registers its highest average temperatures. During the summer months in tropical climates, hurricanes form around a narrow, permanent band of equatorial low pressure called the equatorial trough. In the Northern Hemisphere, the trade winds that blow in from the northeast converge in the equatorial trough.

Once the sun heats a large area of the ocean's surface, the air comes in contact with the water and is warmed by it as well. The warmer air begins expanding and rising more than the cooler air surrounding it. This creates a tropical wave, or an area of low atmospheric pressure. The warmer the air, the lighter it becomes, which makes it exert less, or lower, pressure on the atmosphere. An area of cooler air is heavier, making for higher pressure. Atmospheric pressure is measured by a device called a barometer, so a sharp drop in barometric pressure is an early sign that atmospheric trouble is brewing.

A tropical wave is typically an unorganized mass of rain and thunderstorms, but as it drifts over the warmed tropical waters, it continues to draw in warm, moist air that cools as it rises. As the water vapor cools, it condenses into water droplets that form clouds.

The cooling air also gives off energy in the form of heat as it condenses from a gas (vapor) to a liquid (raindrops). This additional heat also rises, which in turn triggers strong thermal updrafts—fast-rising columns of heated air—that pull the warm air even higher into the atmosphere. This process repeats itself over and over again: warm water rising, cooling, condensing, feeding the tropical wave, and causing it to grow, while excess heat energy draws the warm air higher into the sky.

From Tropical Wave to Tropical Depression

All of this cycling of heat and moisture through the atmosphere will quickly grow into storm clouds that produce a large area of thunderstorms that can last for a day or more. Air flows from areas of high pressure to low pressure in much the same way that water flows downhill. Cooler, heavier air will always rush in to fill the void left by the rising warmer, lighter air. Just as the speed with which water flows downhill depends on

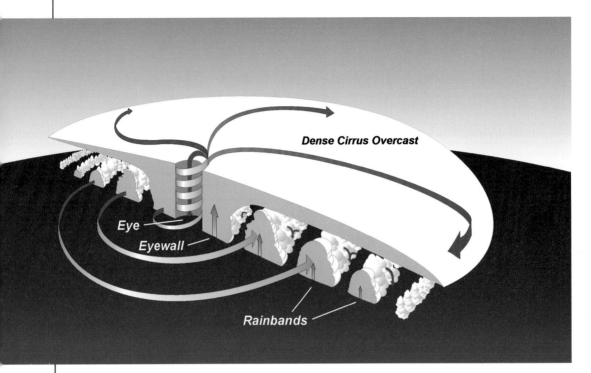

Dense Cirrus Overcast

Eye

Eyewall

Rainbands

This cutaway view of a hurricane shows the bands of clouds and moisture swirling around the eye, or center, of the cyclonic storm.

the steepness of the slope it is descending, the speed with which air travels depends on the extent of the difference between the high- and low-pressure areas.

The air flowing from high pressure to low is what we feel as wind, and the difference between the two areas is known as the pressure-gradient force (PGF). In the Northern Hemisphere, the winds in a low-pressure system will curve, or circle counterclockwise, due to the combined influences of the PGF and the Coriolis force, which is similar to centrifugal force and is a result of the earth's rotation.

A tropical wave that produces thunderstorms for several days and achieves sustained winds of 38 mph (61 km/h) as it moves westward along its equatorial path is upgraded to a tropical disturbance. Some tropical disturbances will continue to grow and strengthen and, when winds hit 73 mph (119 km/h), become tropical storms.

It takes a large amount of energy to nurture and feed a storm. It requires massive, fresh quantities of warm, moist air to be drawn into the growing and rotating mass of air and moisture. Once trapped in the circling system, the air rises into the atmosphere, cooling as it ascends. When the air reaches its maximum height, the cooler air sinks back, returning toward the equator as blowing wind. In fact, it contributes to the phenomenon known as the trade winds (winds that blow almost constantly from the equator toward the northeast). It will also begin to warm up again as it falls, creating a level of air that is warmer than the air below it. This is known as high-level temperature inversion.

In most storms, the inversion layer will limit the height to which the storm clouds can grow by blocking the warm air beneath it from rising any higher. However, some storms grow so fast and so vigorously that strong thermal updrafts from below will break through the inversion layer. When this happens, the storm can grow to monstrous proportions, with driving rain, high winds, and storm clouds swelling up to 40,000 feet (12,192 meters).

A Towering Funnel of Air

As fierce as these storms may be, under certain conditions they possess the potential to grow even larger and more powerful. This requires the presence of an area of high pressure, called an anticyclone, at an altitude of about 56,000 feet (17,969 m). The high pressure might be produced by the rising air of the low-pressure system— called a cyclone—or the remnant of an earlier weather system. In either case, the strong updraft of air will feed and intensify the anticyclone.

In the Northern Hemisphere, air flows clockwise around areas of high pressure and counterclockwise around low pressure. In the Southern Hemisphere, the directions are reversed. Cyclonic circulation is the process in which air is drawn into the low-pressure area near the earth's surface. The pressure differences between high and low areas keep the air moving and accelerating until it can go no faster. Then it rises, spiraling higher into the atmosphere until it meets the anticyclone. The anticyclone's opposite, or clockwise, spin then sweeps the rising counterclockwise air away from the storm's center.

As the rising air is pushed aside, more air is drawn upward to take its place, causing the atmospheric pressure at the surface to drop still lower. By this point in its development, the storm will have grown to some 400 miles (644 km) across, with winds in excess of 74 mph (119 km/h). All the warm, moist air continues to be drawn upward, feeding the storm, acting as a funnel that draws in an endless supply of air and moisture to fuel itself. Just as water going down a drain will form a little whirlpool, or vortex, this air and moisture will swirl in a vortex pattern. This is known as vorticity—when a liquid or gas begins to turn around an axis, like the low-pressure center of a hurricane.

Soon, the air at the center of this towering funnel will be warmer than the air circulating around it. The winds at the center, or the eye, of the hurricane will diminish to 10 mph (16 km/h). The entire 20–30 mile (32–48 km) diameter of the eye will be virtually cloudless and calm, and it will be surrounded by a solid wall of clouds that rises into the sky.

In a matter of days, a simple patch of water warmed by the sun has grown into a ferocious hurricane.

Making Landfall

Most hurricanes form in two narrow bands approximately 5° to 30° latitude north and south of the equator. Hurricanes cannot form in the smaller strip of 5° on either side of the equator because the Coriolis effect there isn't strong enough to give the storm the spin needed to elevate it from tropical wave to hurricane status.

Hurricanes in the Caribbean and western North Atlantic account for about one in six of the storms that sweep the Northern Hemisphere every year. Atlantic hurricanes tend to move west, slowly curving away from the equator to head for the islands of the Caribbean, including Puerto Rico, the Dominican Republic, Haiti, the Bahamas, and Cuba, before swinging into the Gulf of Mexico, Florida, or, on occasion, up the Atlantic seaboard. Atlantic hurricanes have even been known to cross the ocean and reach Europe. In other parts of the world, the tendency is for hurricanes—which are born on the western sides of oceans not far from continents—to move along tracks that take them into inhabited regions.

Whether they are called tropical cyclones, baguio, or typhoons, hurricanes are both frightening and devastating. Even before they make landfall, when the storms are as much as 500 miles (800 km) from shore, their presence can be seen and felt in the long, slow waves that push ahead of them and pound at the shore.

High, feathery cirrus clouds begin to appear, often radiating from a central point on the horizon. Soon, the storm itself comes into view, a mass of dark-gray storm clouds and lower, swifter clouds that move left to right across the sky. Bands of rain begin making landfall

Hurricane Carol surged up the East Coast of the United States in 1954. It made landfall first in North Carolina and then in New York.

while the storm is still some 100 miles (160 km) from the shore, each band bringing increasingly heavier rains and stronger winds.

The hurricane's full fury finally hits, packing winds in excess of 75 mph (120 km/h) that last from two to four hours. Trees are uprooted. Homes are flattened. Automobiles, boats, and railroad cars are lifted and blown hundreds of feet through the air. Windows shatter, roofs are peeled away from houses, and the torrential downpour brings about flash floods.

Along the coast, the sea level can rise as much as 20 feet (6 m) from the storm surge, which is the cause of more death and destruction than even the fierce winds or heavy rains. The low-pressure center of the hurricane draws up a mound of water as much as several feet above the usual sea level and 50 miles (80 km) wide. The center of the storm pushes this mound of water a short distance inland, on average some 20 feet (6 m). In the hurricane that struck Galveston, Texas, in the Gulf of Mexico in 1900, the storm surge raised the water level 4 feet (1.2 m) in just four seconds. Most of the storm's 6,000 deaths were blamed on the surge.

The surge can also bring large breaking waves that are slammed into shore by the winds. These 5- to 10-foot (1.5–3 m) waves can come in and roll back out quickly and without warning, sweeping away people and animals, smashing buildings and boats, eroding coastal areas, and weakening the foundations of buildings and bridges. Flooding from a tropical cyclone that hit the Bay of Bengal in 1991 flooded Bangladesh and caused more than 100,000 deaths.

A hurricane needs a continuous infusion of warm air and water to sustain it. As soon as it leaves warm tropical waters—which are its fuel and the source of its strength—the hurricane begins to slow and weaken. Yet it can still travel great distances over land and cause vast destruction before the storm system falls apart, typically in two to three days.

Rating a Hurricane's Strength and Giving It a Name

The Saffir-Simpson scale divides hurricanes into five categories of increasing severity:

- **Category 1:** The barometric pressure is more than 28.94 inches (on the scale used to measure atmospheric air pressure), with winds of between 74 and 95 mph (119–153 km/h). At this level, trees, bushes, and unanchored objects as large as mobile homes are damaged.

- **Category 2:** The barometer is between 28.50 and 28.91 inches, with winds between 96 and 110 mph (120–177 km/h), strong enough to blow over trees, damage exposed mobile homes, and cause minor damage to roofs.

- **Category 3:** The barometric pressure drops to between 27.91 and 28.47 inches, as the winds blow between 111 and 130 mph (179–209 km/h). These winds will strip the leaves from trees, uproot large trees, destroy mobile homes, and cause structural damage to buildings.

- **Category 4:** The barometer drops to between 27.17 and 27.88 inches, with sustained winds between 131 and 155 mph (211–249 km/h) that can blow down street signs; damage windows, doors, and roofs; cause heavy damage to buildings near the shore; and generate flooding as far as six miles inland.

- **Category 5:** Winds blast at greater than 155 mph (249 km/h), and the barometric pressure drops below 27.17 inches. At those speeds, windows, doors, and roofs sustain heavy damage, small buildings will be completely destroyed, and structures less than 15 feet (4.5 m) above sea level and within 1,500 feet (457 m) of the shore will suffer major damage.

For ease of identification while they are being tracked, all tropical storms are named. In the past, hurricanes had been named after the particular saint's day on which they occurred, or they were identified by their longitude and latitude. These early systems proved confusing, however, especially when more than one storm was in an area at the same time. Military weather forecasters began giving women's names to major storms during World War II (1939–1945), but in 1950 the World Meteorological Organization (WMO) adopted an alphabetical naming system based on military radio code (i.e., "able" means "a," "baker" means "b," "charlie" means "c," and so on). In 1950, Hurricane Able became the first Atlantic hurricane to be named in this manner.

The WMO quickly realized the potential for confusion that its new system would create if two or more powerful Hurricane Ables formed and made landfall at roughly the same time. So, in 1953, the WMO changed the system to a rotating list of women's names. The first significant tropical storm of the season might be Alice, the second Betty, the third Carmen, etc. In a nod to gender equality, the organization added men's names to the list in 1979, rotating them boy-girl-boy-girl (Abe-Betty-Chris-Dolores). In even-numbered years, the first named hurricane is a man's name (like "Arthur"); in odd-numbered years, it's a woman's (like "Ana"). The WMO also added Spanish and French names to the mix, in recognition of the languages of the Caribbean nations affected by Atlantic hurricanes. Because the letters q, u, x, y, and z are not used, there are twenty-one names reserved for each year. That set of names is recycled every six years, minus the names that had been retired and replaced by new ones selected by the WMO.

Historic Hurricanes

Hurricanes are hardly a modern phenomenon. Their power and destructiveness have been recorded and marveled at throughout the ages. In 1099, for example, a hurricane blew into the English Channel, the body of water that divides the island nation of England from the European continent. The storm surge, funneled through the channel, killed more than 100,000 people along the coasts of both England and the western edge of the European continent.

The gods were credited with this typhoon that saved Japan from an invading Mongol fleet in 1281. The Japanese named the storm *kamikaze*, or "divine wind."

Typhoons and Cyclones

In 1281, a typhoon that hit Japan helped decide the outcome of its war against the Mongols, who at the time ruled China and Korea. The Japanese were sure to be overwhelmed by the superior Mongolian army sailing toward the Japanese islands when the typhoon destroyed the enemy fleet. The grateful Japanese called the storm *kamikaze*, or "divine wind." Many believed the storm had been sent by the gods to save Japan, and the event led to a religious revival among the Japanese people.

The typhoon that struck East Pakistan (now Bangladesh) in South Asia on November 13, 1970, proved itself to be the deadliest known tropical cyclone in recorded history. With winds estimated to have exceeded 120 mph (190 km/h), storm surges between 15 and 20 feet (5–6 m) sent a tidal flood into the low-lying coastal areas in the early-morning hours. More than 500,000 people drowned in this catastrophic storm, many of them in their sleep. More than 100,000 people were reported missing in the aftermath. The Bay of Bengal, which lies in the path of the typical Southern Hemisphere cyclone storm route, was hit by another typhoon in 1991, this one claiming 140,000 lives.

Typhoon Tip holds the record for the largest and most powerful tropical cyclone on record. Before it hit Japan on October 19, 1979, it had achieved wind speeds of 161 mph (258 km/h), was spread across a radius of 675 miles (1,085 km), and had sustained gale force winds across a diameter of 1,350 miles (2,170 km). On average, most tropical cyclones hold together for a week to ten days. However, Tip formed in the northwestern Pacific Ocean on October 4 and became a typhoon two days later. It reached its peak on October 12 and made landfall, much weakened, on the Japanese island of Honshu on the 19th. Though far from the height of its power by the time it made landfall, Tip still managed to cause considerable damage, including sixty-eight deaths and millions of dollars worth of damage to the Japanese fishing and agricultural industries.

Cyclone Catarina is the first storm to be positively identified as a tropical cyclone to form in the typically cool waters of the South Atlantic. It struck Brazil on March 27, 2004. Catarina slowly developed into a tropical cyclone before attaining winds of 110 mph (180 km/h). The cyclone killed three and caused some $350 million in property destruction, including damaging 40,000 homes and destroying 1,500. It also destroyed three-quarters of the country's banana crop and 40 percent of its rice output.

Florida and the Gulf Coast

Because it juts out into both the Atlantic and the Gulf of Mexico, Florida lies directly in the path of Caribbean hurricanes. Hardly a year goes by when Florida and/or the Gulf coasts of Texas, Mississippi, Louisiana, and Alabama are not struck by at least one storm.

A hurricane that struck Galveston, Texas, on September 8,

A powerful storm surge, crashing waves, and Category 2–force winds devastated the barrier island city of Galveston in 1900.

1900, remains the deadliest natural disaster in American history. Despite warnings from the U.S. Weather Bureau, the citizens of Galveston made little effort to evacuate or prepare their exposed barrier island for the coming onslaught. The storm surge swept across the 3-mile-wide (5 km) barrier island that separates Galveston Bay from the Gulf of Mexico. Galveston is a port city and lies about 4.5 feet (1.3 m) above sea level. The 4-foot (1.2 m) surge submerged bridges connecting the city to the mainland, and crashing waves destroyed waterfront buildings and homes. Billions of tons of water swept across the city, pushed by winds gusting up to 100 mph (160 km/h), smashing anything the winds might have left standing.

Despite warnings from the U.S. Weather Bureau, the citizens of Galveston made little effort to evacuate . . . Six thousand people were killed, and 5,000 were injured.

In all, 2,600 homes were destroyed, and 10,000 people—one-quarter of the population—were left homeless. Six thousand people were killed, and 5,000 were injured.

The city was flattened, but Galveston managed to rebuild, erecting a 17-foot-high (5 m), 10-mile-long (16 km) sea wall to protect itself from future hurricanes. The next hurricane to strike Galveston, in August 1915, brought with it a 12-foot (3.6 m) surge that flooded the city with six feet (2 m) of water in some places and killed 275 people. Another,

In 1992, Hurricane Andrew left more than 250,000 people homeless across Florida and Louisiana.

even more powerful hurricane struck in September 1961, but the sea wall did its job and less than fifty lives were claimed by the storm.

One of the worst storms in Florida's history was the Labor Day storm of 1935. It hit southern Florida with winds estimated to have been between 150 and 200 mph (241–322 km/h), although no instruments could get an accurate measurement. The storm was sustained by a low-pressure system at its center with the lowest barometric pressure ever recoded in the Western Hemisphere up to that time. In 1988, this record was broken when Hurricane Gilbert registered a barometric pressure of 26.13 inches. The average pressure at sea level is 29.92 inches.

On August 24, 1992, Hurricane Andrew slammed into Florida, sweeping over Homestead and parts of Miami before continuing on across the Gulf of Mexico and hitting the coast of Louisiana. Until 2005's Hurricane Katrina, Andrew was the costliest natural disaster in American history. Fifteen people died, and the intense rains, tidal surges, and winds left 250,000 people homeless and 82,000 businesses damaged or destroyed. Environmental damage included 33 percent of the coral reefs at Biscayne National Park and 90 percent of South Dade's native pinelands, mangroves, and tropical hardwood hammocks. The damage to Florida and the Gulf Coast caused by Andrew cost some $21 million. The storm produced trash and debris that were equivalent to thirty-years' worth of average trash accumulation.

The Eastern Seaboard

Though relatively uncommon, hurricanes do sometimes veer north to travel up the eastern seaboard of the United States, sometimes rolling as far north as Canada. The most famous of these northern hurricanes was the storm that struck on Labor Day, 1938. It smashed across Long Island, New York, and claimed more than 600 lives as it plowed through homes and businesses, uprooting trees and tossing automobiles and boats around like toys. By the time the storm reached Massachusetts, traveling along the Atlantic Coast at a brisk 56 mph (90 km/h), it was sustaining winds of 121 mph (195 km/h) and gusting up to 183 mph (295 km/h).

Long Island and parts of New England were flattened by the "New England Hurricane" of 1938, a northeast-tracking storm.

New England is no stranger to either nor'easters (ocean storms that feature strong cyclonic winds from the northeast) or hurricanes. The region has suffered through hurricanes in 1944, 1954, 1955, 1960, 1972, 1976, and 1979. In 1954 alone, the Northeast was hit by three major storms: Hurricane Carol, the most damaging storm to strike the region up to that time, in August; Edna in September; and the giant, 9,000-square-mile (14,484 sq km) Hurricane Hazel in October. Even before reaching North America, Hazel killed more than 1,000 people in Haiti and drenched Puerto Rico—500 miles (805 km) to the east—with 12 inches (30.5 cm) of rain. It made landfall at Myrtle Beach, South Carolina, on October 15, with a storm surge of 17 feet (5 m).

3 Hurricane Katrina

Since records have been kept, the United States has only been struck by three Category 5 hurricanes: 1935's Labor Day storm that hit the Florida Keys; Hurricane Camille, which struck Mississippi, Louisiana, and Virginia in 1969; and Hurricane Andrew, which ravaged Florida and Louisiana in 1992.

Hurricane Katrina was the eleventh named storm of the 2005 season, the fifth hurricane and third major hurricane of what was turning out to be an unusually busy hurricane season. Katrina formed as Tropical Depression Twelve over the

This satellite view of 2005's Hurricane Katrina shows the storm over southeastern Louisiana, when it was at Category 4 status.

southeastern Bahamas on August 23, 2005. It began as an interaction between a tropical wave and the remnants of an earlier system, Tropical Depression Ten. The next day, the tropical depression was upgraded to Tropical Storm Katrina. It did not gain enough intensity to become a hurricane until hours before making landfall on the eastern coast of Florida, between Hallandale Beach and Adventura.

Cut off from the warm ocean waters needed to sustain it, Katrina began weakening over land. However, it regained strength within hours of hitting the warm waters of the Gulf of Mexico after passing over Florida's west coast. By Saturday, August 27, Katrina was reinvigorated and stronger than ever, reaching Category 3 status. The storm continued to grow and intensify, nearly doubling in size in the Gulf and becoming a Category 5 hurricane at noon on August 28, with maximum sustained winds of 175 mph (280 km/h).

Katrina made landfall early on the morning of Monday, August 29, as a Category 3 storm near Buras-Triumph, Louisiana. It featured sustained winds of 125 mph (205 km/h) that blasted across southeast Louisiana and Breton Sound before making its third and final landfall on the Louisiana/Mississippi border. Katrina traveled more than 150 miles (240 km) inland to Jackson, Mississippi, where, without the fuel of warm water to feed it and further weakened by the friction it encountered while traveling over land, it began to exhaust its incredible power. Katrina was downgraded to a tropical depression near Clarksville, Tennessee. The last of the killer storm disappeared into a weather front in the eastern Great Lakes region on August 31.

The Eve of Destruction

The city of New Orleans lies on the Gulf of Mexico around a curve of the Mississippi River. The city is surrounded by water. Lake Pontchartrain lies just to the north and connects to Lake Borgne, which in turn opens on the Gulf of Mexico. Lakes, marshlands, and bayous extend outward in all directions from the city, some parts of which lie about 5 to 10 feet (1.5–3 m) below sea level. Lake Pontchartrain's surface is normally about 2 feet (0.6 km) above sea level, and its waters are ordinarily contained by a system of levees and a 14-foot (4.2 m) high floodwall built by the U.S. Army Corps of Engineers. The city, then, lies in what amounts to a shallow bowl surrounded by water.

As Katrina continued its easterly passage across Florida and into the Gulf, forecasters were predicting the storm would make landfall along the Louisiana coast, most likely around New Orleans. As the hurricane blasted toward the city on Sunday, August 28, with winds of 160 mph (257.5 km/h), a mandatory evacuation order was issued. New Orleans Mayor Ray Nagin correctly predicted that, "We are facing a storm that most of us have long feared. This is a once-in-a-lifetime event." Indeed it was; Louisiana had not been hit by a major storm since Hurricane Betty in 1965.

With a population of 485,000 and only one highway leading out of town, New Orleans could not hope to evacuate everyone before Katrina hit. According to an August 29, 2005, report in the *New York Times*, "Many in

An estimated 18,000 cars an hour were evacuating New Orleans as Hurricane Katrina approached. The Superdome appears in the background. It would soon serve as the nation's largest storm shelter and refugee center.

New Orleans, including stranded tourists, stayed behind, with as many as 10,000 of them crowding into the Superdome arena, which the city designated as a shelter of last resort. People five and six abreast waited in line for hours to get into the arena, clutching children, blankets and pillows, oversize pieces of luggage, or plastic bags filled with belongings."

U.S. president George W. Bush declared a state of emergency for the regions that were expected to be ravaged by Katrina, including Louisiana, Mississippi, Alabama, and Florida. Airlines cancelled all flights in and out of the threatened region, stranding tens of thousands of tourists who sought refuge in hotels, along with many local residents seeking rooms above ground level to escape the coming floods. The Federal Emergency Management Agency (FEMA), the government agency responsible for managing crisis situations, began to move emergency supplies, personnel, and equipment into the area, including water, ice, and Meals Ready to Eat (MRE; rations ordinarily served to deployed soldiers).

According to the *New York Times*, "Louisiana state officials said that at one point during the evacuation of New Orleans on Sunday, more than 18,000 cars an hour were leaving the city." Across the region, government officials were fearing the worst. Louisiana Governor Kathleen Babineaux Blanco said, "I think this storm is bigger than anything we have dealt with before. This is not a minor problem." Robert R. Latham Jr., the director of Emergency Management Operations for Mississippi, said, "I'm afraid this is the one we've dreaded. I don't think the scenario could be any worse for us."

In Gulfport, Mississippi, 55 miles (89 km) east of New Orleans, residents could not help but be reminded of 1969's Hurricane Camille, which blasted through their city with 200 mph (322 km/h) winds that killed 250 people across three states. Gulfport officials urged residents to evacuate, fearing that many of the local buildings desig-nated as emergency shelters would not be able to withstand Katrina's 150 mph (241 km/h) winds.

Mobile, Alabama, expected a storm surge higher than any it had ever previously experienced—as much as 20 feet (6 m)—that would flood its historic downtown district. As far east as the Florida Panhandle, residents

Even weeks after Hurricane Katrina had spent its fury, parts of New Orleans remained flooded until the city's levees could be repaired.

were urged to evacuate as the storm waters flooded coastal roads and endangered homes.

Broken Levees

When Katrina finally struck the Gulf Coast just after 6 AM on Monday, August 29, the results were even more devastating than expected. New Orleans was spared the direct hit some had predicted as Katrina came ashore several miles south of the city at Buras-Triumph, Louisiana. Though the storm had by then been downgraded from Category 5 to Category 4, the small 5-square-mile (8 sq km) community of less than 3,400 people was devastated by the storm, which flattened homes and businesses. After Buras-Triumph absorbed Katrina's initial hit, New Orleans was next in the storm's sights. The city was pounded by 145 mph (233 km/h) winds for eight straight hours.

By late in the day, Katrina's fury had passed through New Orleans, but any sense of relief was misplaced. The historic city's troubles were just beginning. It was not the rain from the hurricane that flooded the city and surrounding areas. Rather, it was the water of Lake Pontchartrain that first overran, then broke through, the levees that were supposed to keep the floodwaters at bay. According to a report in the *New York Times* on August 31, 2005, "Streets that were essentially dry in the hours immediately after the hurricane passed were several feet deep in water on Tuesday morning. Even downtown areas that lie on higher ground were flooded . . . [B]oth city airports were underwater."

The levees that had been built to withstand 13 feet (4 m) of water were overwhelmed by floodwaters that rose to more than 17 feet (5 m). As the storm moved over Lake Borgne to the east, an estimated 18-foot (5.5 m) storm surge washed over the levees that were designed to protect the area around the lake.

The system of levees, floodwalls, storm gates, and pumps that was supposed to keep the Mississippi River and the waters of Lake Pontchartrain in check were not up to the task of containing Katrina's fury. They had been designed to protect against flooding from fast-moving Category 3 storms. Katrina's more slow-moving fury was simply too much for the levees to withstand. In the wake of the storm, stories also emerged that the levees and floodwalls were not as well constructed as they were supposed to be by the Corps of Engineers and didn't meet the Corps' own design specifications.

The waters of the Mississippi River and Lake Pontchartrain surged over the levees and flooded 80 percent of the city, devastating St. Bernard's Parish, east New Orleans, and the Ninth Ward in particular. On the southern shore of Lake Pontchartrain, entire communities of single-story homes were flooded to their rooftops.

A City Destroyed and a Region Devastated

Nearly one million residents were without electricity and telephone service as power lines snapped and utility poles were knocked down. Cellular phone towers were damaged or toppled. Several parishes—or counties—were described by Governor Blanco as having been devastated by high winds and floodwaters. In one, St. Bernard's Parish, some 40,000 homes were flooded, and the

Residents of New Orleans's Lower Ninth Ward—one of the city's hardest-hit and poorest neighborhoods—await rescue from the floodwaters in the aftermath of Hurricane Katrina.

emergency center was underwater. In New Orleans, a 15-foot (4.5 m) section of the Superdome's roof—where some 10,000 refugees from the storm huddled for protection—was peeled away. Conditions in the Superdome and the city's Convention Center—also serving as an emergency shelter—deteriorated as temperatures soared, water supplies were depleted, food became scarce, and human waste began collecting. Mostly false rumors of violence within the Superdome and Convention Center, including rapes and murders, began circulating, and panic took hold.

Bridges were washed out, and highways were made impassable by the floodwaters. The Pentagon ordered navy ships, maritime rescue teams, and helicopters to the Gulf Coast to help with the rescue operation and evacuate people from the roofs of homes, where they fled to escape the rising waters. Meanwhile, in New Orleans, drowned bodies were found in the streets, floating through deluged neighborhoods, and in the attics of flooded houses. Looting and gun violence were widespread, and many from the city's police force either abandoned their posts or didn't report for duty.

Previously, 1992's Hurricane Andrew held the record as the costliest tropical cyclone in terms of economic and property damage, causing $21 billion in losses. The storm also killed fifteen people. In comparison, Katrina was responsible for some 1,500 deaths and more than $25 billion in damages across Louisiana, Texas, and the rest of the Gulf Coast. The cost to the federal government for cleanup, repair, and reconstruction of the affected areas is believed to be $105 billion. The hurricane destroyed an estimated 200,000 homes, disrupted oil production in the Gulf Coast, and created hundreds of thousands of refugees, mostly from hard-hit New Orleans. As of February 2006, fully three-quarters of the city's population had yet to return to their homes.

The 2005 Hurricane Season

From 1900 through 2004, the U.S. coast from Texas to Maine has been hit by 174 hurricanes, most of which were Category 3 or lower. Florida has taken almost twice as many direct hits from hurricanes (sixty-four) as second-place Texas (thirty-eight). Louisiana, which suffered through twenty-seven hurricanes during that period, lags behind North Carolina with its twenty-nine hits. Only sixteen Category 4 and two Category 5 storms were recorded during that entire period. Yet in the 2005 hurricane season, the Atlantic and

Gulf coasts saw four Category 5 storms, including pre-landfall Hurricane Katrina. Was this random chance? Bad luck? Or is something going on to create more numerous and powerful tropical storms?

Hurricanes appear to go through cycles of greater and lesser intensity roughly every twenty to thirty years. For example, the Atlantic experienced an above-average number of storms during the 1940s through the 1960s. This period included some of the most deadly and costly tropical storms on record in 1944, 1954, 1955 (Hurricane Diane), 1957 (Hurricane Audrey), 1960, 1963 (Hurricane Flora), and 1965 (Hurricane Betsy). Between 1971 and 1994, however, the North Atlantic hurricane season averaged only about eight named storms, five hurricanes, and one major hurricane a year.

Only sixteen Category 4 and two Category 5 storms were recorded between 1900 and 2004. Yet in the 2005 hurricane season, the Atlantic and Gulf coasts saw four Category 5 storms, including pre-landfall Hurricane Katrina.

According to a late 2005 report by the National Oceanic and Atmospheric Administration (NOAA), the agency that tracks weather and climate conditions around the world:

The nation is now wrapping up the eleventh year of a new era of heightened Atlantic hurricane activity. This era has been unfolding in the Atlantic since 1995 and is expected to continue for the next decade or perhaps longer. NOAA attributes this increased activity to natural occurring cycles in tropical climate patterns near the equator. These cycles, called "the tropical multi-decadal signal," typically last several decades (twenty to thirty years, or even longer). As a result, the North Atlantic experiences alternating decades long (twenty- to thirty-year periods, or even longer) of above-normal or below-normal hurricane seasons.

Prior to this cycle of increased activity, the United States would experience an average of only two to three major hurricanes making landfall in any given season. Since 2002, a total of twenty-nine named storms have hit this country, an average of seven storms per season. Twenty of these have struck the Gulf Coast, and nine have hit the East Coast. Thirteen of the named storms were hurricanes, of which eight made landfall along the Gulf states.

Hurricane Rita

As destructive as Hurricane Katrina was in 2005, it was far from the end of what would be one of the worst

Texas residents were hit by the 2005 hurricane season's third Category 5 storm in late September when Hurricane Rita made landfall near the Texas-Louisiana border.

hurricane seasons on record. Hurricane Katrina was just the start of a very bad year for Louisiana and the rest of the Gulf Coast. Less than three weeks after Katrina swept across Florida, Louisiana, and Mississippi, Hurricane Rita began to form as the season's eighteenth tropical depression in the North Atlantic on September 17. It became the 2005 Atlantic hurricane season's seventeenth named storm, its tenth hurricane, fifth major hurricane, and third Category 5 hurricane. Within a day of its formation, it was upgraded to a tropical storm. By September 20, it was packing winds of 75 mph (121 km/h) and had become a Category 1 hurricane.

Rita's path took it across the Bahamas and Cuba. Upon hitting the waters of the Gulf of Mexico—warmer than usual for late September—it began to pick up speed and intensity. By mid-afternoon on September 21, it was declared a Category 5 storm, with sustained winds of 165 mph (265 km/h). That night, it reached its maximum intensity. Packing ferocious 180 mph (290 km/h) winds, it sped toward the already beleaguered and battered Gulf Coast.

Rita finally made landfall between Sabine Pass, Texas, and Johnson's Bayou, Louisiana, in the early-morning hours of September 24. It hit land as a Category 3 Hurricane, with winds of 115 mph (185 km/h). The storm finally blew itself out in the lower Mississippi Valley. It was absorbed into a cold front on the morning of September 26, but not before

Route 87 in Port Arthur, Texas, is completely submerged under record floodwaters following the exit of Hurricane Rita.

spawning tornados from the system's outer band that claimed both lives and property in Arkansas.

In all, Hurricane Rita was responsible for 120 deaths and an estimated $10 billion in damages across the Bahamas, Cuba, the Yucatán Peninsula of Mexico, Florida, Louisiana, Texas, Mississippi, and Arkansas. Though not as deadly as Hurricane Katrina, Rita was nonetheless the fourth most intense Atlantic storm on record and was the most intense hurricane ever to form in the Atlantic basin. Only its path and speed kept it from inflicting even greater damage than Katrina, though its storm surge did cause another failure in the already weakened New Orleans levee system, resulting in major reflooding in that city.

Hurricane Wilma

Even after the exit of Rita, the 2005 hurricane season was not finished breaking records and wreaking havoc across the Atlantic and the Gulf of Mexico. On October 15, the twenty-fourth tropical depression of the season formed in the North Atlantic. By October 17, it had become a tropical storm and was named Wilma, the first time a "w" name had been used since alphabetical naming began in 1950. This made 2005 the most active hurricane season since the twenty-one storms of 1933.

The historic town of Key West, Florida, is flooded by Hurricane Wilma in October 2005, the end of the most active hurricane season in the United States since 1933.

When it was upgraded to a hurricane on October 18, Wilma was the season's twelfth hurricane, tying the record set in 1969 for the most hurricanes in one season. It was only the third Category 5 hurricane ever to develop in the month of October. It was the twenty-second storm, thirteenth hurricane, sixth major hurricane, and fourth Category 5 hurricane of that record-breaking season. Wilma also produced the fastest and greatest

Hurricane Wilma pounded western Cuba after charging through Mexico's Yucatán Peninsula. Half a million Cubans were evacuated to higher ground.

drop in air pressure ever recorded. It would reach Category 5 status with maximum sustained winds of 185 mph (295 km/h).

Wilma made several landfalls, including in the Yucatán Peninsula, as a Category 4 storm before drifting north to enter the Gulf of Mexico as a Category 2 hurricane. The waves kicked up by the storm caused severe coastal flooding in Cuba. By the time it passed over the Florida Keys, it had regained much of its strength, thanks to the still-warm waters of the Gulf of Mexico. By the time Wilma made its second landfall at Everglades City, Florida, on the morning of October 24, it was again a Category 3 hurricane. It weakened slightly as it passed over the Florida peninsula.

Once in the Atlantic after its assault on Florida, Wilma roared back to Category 3 strength just north of the Bahamas, absorbing the strength of another nearby tropical storm as it went. It swept up the eastern seaboard, gradually weakening. On the afternoon of October 25, south of Nova Scotia and still packing hurricane winds of 90 mph (145 km/h), it was absorbed by an even larger weather system that at last ended its record-setting journey. In all, Hurricane Wilma was responsible for sixty-two deaths and an estimated $12 billion in damages in the United States alone.

The worst Atlantic hurricane season in human memory had come to an end.

Increasing Hurricane Activity and the Future of Killer Storms

The causes of the heightened hurricane activity in the Atlantic Ocean and Gulf of Mexico are still being debated. The National Oceanic and Atmospheric Administration's (NOAA) 2005 report on the subject states, "NOAA research shows that the tropical multi-decadal signal is causing the increased Atlantic hurricane activity since 1995, and is not related to greenhouse warming." NOAA believes that a normal cycle of increasing and decreasing hurricane intensity is at work here, not climate change. Its studies have shown that the conditions that result in more intense hurricanes—warmer waters and favorable tropical winds from Africa—have been in place since 1995. "With an active hurricane era comes many more landfalling tropical storms, hurricanes, and major hurricanes in the United States," the report continues. "Since 2002, the country has experienced an average of seven landfalling tropical storms and hurricanes per season. The United States can expect ongoing high levels of landfalling tropical storms and hurricanes while we remain in this active era."

Other experts such as Judith Curry, an atmospheric scientist at the Georgia Institute of Technology in Atlanta, disagree and place the blame not on natural cycles, but on human causes. Curry pointed specifically to the generation of greenhouse gases and the resulting increase in atmospheric temperature. In a report on her findings published on NationalGeographic.com, Curry said, "Global warming is sending sea-surface temperatures up, so we're looking at an increase in hurricane intensity globally."

Whatever the cause, there is little debate that the frequency and severity of hurricanes have increased, and they will continue to do so in the coming years. Estimates for the 2006 season varied, but experts at Colorado State University forecast seventeen tropical storms, of which nine would be expected to become hurricanes and five would be major hurricanes. The National Hurricane Center predicted sixteen named storms for the period, with six of

New York City has been hit by sixteen tropical storms in the last century, including 1960's Hurricane Donna, pictured above. Donna resulted in the deaths of fifty people in the United States.

them developing into major hurricanes. A week prior to the start of the 2006 hurricane season, NOAA forecast thirteen to sixteen named storms, with eight to ten expected to become hurricanes over the following six months. Luckily, the season turned out to be far quieter than expected.

Potentially Catastrophic Vulnerabilities

Increased hurricane activity means danger for not only traditional high-risk areas such as Florida, the Gulf

Coast, and North Carolina's Outer Banks, but for the rest of the eastern seaboard as well. New York City, for example, is no stranger to hurricanes. The New York metropolitan area has been hit by sixteen tropical storms and hurricanes since 1900, and lies directly in the path of any storm riding up the eastern seaboard. According to an article on NationalGeographic.com from May 2006, "A 1990 study by the U.S. Army Corps of Engineers said the three U.S. cities most vulnerable to hurricanes are New Orleans, Miami, and New York."

The worst hurricane on record to strike the New York area was the September 1938 Long Island storm that hit with sustained winds exceeding 120 miles an hour (193 km/h). The last major hurricane to hit New York was Donna in September 1960. Donna created an 11-foot (3.3 m) storm surge that caused extensive damage to the piers in New York Harbor and forced the evacuation of hundreds of families along the Long Island coast.

Sheltered by New York Harbor and Long Island Sound, the city is unlikely to take a direct hit from a hurricane. But even a storm centered nearby could create surges that swamp large parts of the city and Long Island. John F. Kennedy Airport on Jamaica Bay could find itself underwater, as could lower Manhattan, depending on the angle of the storm's approach and whether it struck at high or low tide. The high winds of

This computer simulation shows the potentially deadly storm surge and catastrophic flooding that would accompany a powerful hurricane striking Manhattan.

a Category 4 or 5 hurricane could also prove disastrous to the city's innumerable skyscrapers, many of which were never intended to withstand the battering forces of 130 mph-plus (209 km/h) gales.

In the event of a severe hurricane in New York, one of the biggest risks to human life and catastrophic damage lies underground in the city's subway system. According to a report published on LiveScience.com, "Exacerbating [increasing and intensifying] the risk, subways and other tunnels that connect to each other can funnel floodwater to unexpected places. And a disaster underground could cause the collapse of structures that support the floors above." In September 2004, the remnants of Hurricane Frances hit New York and flooded some subway tunnels, stranding passengers aboard trains stalled on flooded tracks. A more severe storm, accompanied by high storm surges, could drown those same tunnels. Additionally, the New York metropolitan area is home to

> *The New York metropolitan area is home to almost 20 million people, a number that would be virtually impossible to evacuate with even the most advanced warning.*

almost 20 million people, a number that would be virtually impossible to evacuate with even the most advanced warning of an approaching storm.

In addition to the physical damage and loss of life a Category 5 hurricane would cause in New York, there is the global economic impact to consider. Hurricane Katrina—along with Wilma and Rita—interrupted oil production in the Gulf of Mexico, directly leading to the sharp increase in gasoline prices that followed. If New York, one of the world's leading financial centers, was underwater and without functioning electricity, communications, and transportation for a prolonged period of time, the effect on the world's economy would be disastrous. According to the United States Landfalling Hurricane Probability Project, there is a 30 percent probability that New York City or Long Island will be hit by a tropical storm or hurricane in 2006, and a 73 percent probability that such an event will happen sometime in the next fifty years.

The Bottom Line

Humankind cannot hope to prevent hurricanes or turn them aside from their paths of death and destruction. All that we can do is improve our ability to accurately forecast and track the formation and progress of tropical cyclones. We must also create viable evacuation plans, improve the infrastructures of coastal areas to enable them to better withstand future storms, and create better and faster emergency response systems and relief efforts.

Unless we meet these urgent needs of all those communities along the vulnerable Gulf Coast and eastern seaboard—not to mention in other locations around the world endangered by cyclones, typhoons, and baguios—we are destined to witness again and again the horrific events of summer 2005, with its televised images of flooded cities, stranded homeowners, frantic refugees, lawlessness, and floating bodies. As the most technologically advanced, wealthiest nation of the world—indeed, of all history—we can, and must, do better to protect those who get caught in the path of nature's wrath.

Glossary

barometric pressure The weight of the atmosphere over a unit area of the earth's surface.

Coriolis force A force exerted on a parcel of air due to the rotation of the earth. This force causes a deflection of air to the right in the Northern Hemisphere and to the left in the Southern Hemisphere.

equatorial trough The low-pressure area that circles the globe along the equator, a result of intense convection, or circulation of the air in which warm air rises and cool air sinks.

eye The center of a tropical storm or hurricane that has low pressure, light winds, and rain-free skies.

eyewall An organized band of thunderstorms surrounding the eye, or center, of a tropical cyclone. Severe thunderstorms, heavy precipitation, and the strongest winds exist in this area.

global warming A gradual warming of the earth's atmosphere generally believed to be caused by the burning of fossil fuels and industrial pollutants.

levees Raised embankments erected to keep waters contained in lakes or rivers.

meteorology The scientific study of the physics, chemistry, and dynamics of the earth's atmosphere, especially weather and climate.

pressure-gradient force The flow of air from an area of high pressure to an area of low pressure.

Saffir-Simpson scale A method of measuring the damage potential and intensity of a hurricane using a scale of 1 to 5.

storm surge An abnormal rise in sea level accompanying a hurricane or other intense storm that can be 20 feet (6 m) high at its peak and 50 to 100 miles (80 to 161 km) wide.

thermal updrafts Fast-rising columns of heated air that pull warm air higher into the atmosphere.

tropical cyclone A general term for all storms that feature cyclonic circulation around a low-pressure system, high winds, and heavy rains originating over tropical waters. Also known as a hurricane (in the North Atlantic and Caribbean), cyclone (Indian Ocean), baguio (Indonesia), and typhoon (Pacific Ocean).

tropical disturbance An unorganized mass of clouds, showers, and thunderstorms that is generally 100 to 300 miles (161 to 482 km) in diameter and develops in the tropics or subtropics.

tropical wave An area of relatively low pressure moving westward through the trade wind easterlies. It is associated with extensive cloudiness and showers, and may indicate tropical cyclone development.

vorticity A measure of the amount of rotation in the atmosphere.

For More Information

Federal Emergency Management Agency (FEMA)
500 C Street SW
Washington, DC 20472
(800) 621-FEMA (3362)
Web site: http://www.fema.gov

Louisiana State University Hurricane Center
Suite 3221, CEBA Building
Baton Rouge, LA 70803
(225) 578-4813
Web site: http://www.hurricane.lsu.edu

National Center for Atmospheric Research & the
  University Cooperative for Atmospheric Research
P.O. Box 3000
Boulder, CO 80307-3000
(303) 497-1000
Web site: http://www.ucar.edu

National Oceanic and Atmospheric Administration (NOAA)
Atlantic Oceanographic and Meteorological
  Laboratory
4301 Rickenbacker Causeway
Miami, FL 33149

(305) 361-4450
Web site: http://www.aoml.noaa.gov/hrd

NOAA National Hurricane Center
Tropical Prediction Center
11691 SW 17th Street
Miami, FL 33165-2149
Web site: http://www.nhc.noaa.gov

NOAA National Weather Service
1325 East-West Highway
Silver Spring, MD 20910
Web site: http://www.nws.noaa.gov

NOAA Office of Oceanic and Atmospheric Research
Silver Spring Metro Center, Bldg. 3, Rm. 11627
1315 East-West Highway
Silver Spring, MD 20910
(301) 713-2458
Web site: http://www.research.noaa.gov

U.S. Geological Survey (USGS)
Coastal and Marine Geology Program
USGS National Center, MS 915
12201 Sunrise Valley Drive
Reston, VA 20192
Web site: http://marine.usgs.gov

Web Sites

Due to the changing nature of Internet links, Rosen Publishing has developed an online list of Web sites related to the subject of this book. This site is updated regularly. Please use this link to access the list:

http://www.rosenlinks.com/in/hurr

For Further Reading

Challoner, Jack. *Hurricane & Tornado*. New York, NY: DK Children, 2004.

Davis, Pete. *Hurricane: Face to Face with Nature's Deadliest Storms*. New York, NY: Owl Books, 2001.

Norcross, Bryan. *Hurricane Almanac 2006: The Essential Guide to Storms Past, Present, and Future*. New York, NY: St. Martin's Griffin, 2006.

Palser, Barb. *Hurricane Katrina: Aftermath of Disaster (Snapshots in History)*. Minneapolis, MN: Compass Point Books, 2006.

Reed, Jim, and Mike Theiss. *Hurricane Katrina: Through the Eyes of Storm Chasers*. Helena, MT: Farcountry Press, 2005.

Sherrow, Victoria. *Hurricane Andrew: Nature's Rage (American Disasters)*. Berkeley Heights, NJ: Enslow Publishers, 1998.

Time Magazine, eds. *Hurricane Katrina: The Storm that Changed America.* New York, NY: *Time* Magazine, 2005.

Williams, Jack. *Hurricane Watch: Forecasting the Deadliest Storms on Earth*. New York, NY: Vantage, 2001.

Bibliography

Allaby, Michael. *Dangerous Weather: Hurricanes*. New York, NY: Facts On File, 1997.

Britt, Robert Roy. "Subway Flooding: A Hidden and Neglected Risk." LiveScience.com. January 14, 2005. Retrieved May 2006 (http://www.livescience.com/forcesofnature/050114_underground_floods.html).

Carruth, Gorton. *What Happened When*. New York, NY: Harper & Row, 1989.

Emanuel, Kerry. *Divine Wind: The History and Science of Hurricanes*. New York, NY: Oxford University Press, 2005.

Lee, Sally. *Hurricanes*. New York, NY: Franklin Watts, 1993.

Mandia, Scott A. "The Long Island Express: The Great Hurricane of 1938: What's in Store for New York's Future?" SUNYSuffolk.edu. Retrieved May 2006 (http://www2.sunysuffolk.edu/mandias/38hurricane/hurricane_future.html).

"NOAA Attributes Recent Increase in Hurricane Activity to Naturally Occurring Multi-Decadal Climate Variability." *NOAA Magazine*, November 29, 2005. Retrieved May 2006 (http://www.magazine.noaa.gov/stories/mag184.htm).

Roach, John. "Warming Oceans Are Fueling Stronger Hurricanes, Study Finds." NationalGeographic.com.

March 16, 2006. Retrieved May 2006 (http://
news.nationalgeographic.com/news/2006/03/
0316_060316_hurricanes.html).

Souza, D. M. *Hurricanes*. Minneapolis, MN: Carolrhoda
Books, 1996.

Treaster, Joseph B., and Abby Goodnough. "Hurricane
Katrina: The Overview: Powerful Storm Threatens
Havoc Along Gulf Coast," *New York Times*, August
29, 2005, sec. A., p. 1.

Treaster, Joseph B., and N. R. Kleinfield. "Hurricane
Katrina: The Overview: New Orleans Is Inundated as
2 Levees Fail; Much of Gulf Coast Is Crippled; Toll
Rises," *New York Times*, August 31, 2005, sec. A., p. 1.

Index

About the Author

Paul Kupperberg is a New York–based writer who works for a national weekly newspaper. He has specialized in science and technology subjects and has written books on aerospace, spy satellites, robotics, and the history of technology. He lives in Connecticut with his wife, Robin, and his son, Max.

Photo Credits

Cover (top left) © James Nielsen/AFP/Getty Images; cover (top right) © Mario Tama/Getty Images; cover (middle left) © Robert Sullivan/AFP/Getty Images; cover (middle right) © Kyle Niemi/U.S. Coast Guard/Getty Images; cover (bottom) © National Hurricane Center/AFP/Getty Images; pp. 3 (left), 4 (top) Jacques Descloitres, MODIS Rapid Response Team, NASA/GSFC; pp. 3 (right), 20 (top) © Bob Pearson/AFP/Getty Images; p. 4 (middle) ©Tim Sloan/AFP/Getty Images; pp. 4 (bottom), 20 (middle), 27 NOAA; p. 5 Earth from Space/NASA; p. 6 © Joe Raedle/Getty Images; p. 10 National Weather Service; p. 15 © NOAA/Photo Researchers, Inc.; p. 20 (bottom) © Photri/Topham/The Image Works; p. 21 © AAAC/Topham/The Image Works; p. 23 © Underwood & Underwood/Corbis; p. 25 © Corbis Sygma; p. 28 (top, middle) Jocelyn Augustino/FEMA; p. 28 (bottom) Master Sgt. Bill Huntington/U.S. Air Force; p. 29 © NOAA/Getty Images; p. 32 © AP/Wide World Photos; p. 34 Bob McMillan/FEMA; p. 37 © Marko Georgiev/Getty Images; p. 39 (top, middle) © Carlo Allegri/Getty Images; pp. 39 (bottom), 42, 43 © Scott Olson/Getty Images; p. 45 © Josh Ritchie/Getty Images; p. 46 © Antonio Levy/AFP/Getty Images; p. 48 (top) © Peter Essick/Aurora/Getty Images; p. 48 (middle) © Atlantide Phototravel/Corbis; p. 48 (bottom) © Steve Liss/Time Life Pictures/Getty Images; p. 50 © Keystone/Getty Images; p. 52 NYC Office of Emergency Management.

Designer: Thomas Forget; Photo Researcher: Amy Feinberg